A Jesse Steam

The Question of the
Vomit Vortex

**Written & Illustrated
by Ken Bowser**

Solving Mysteries Through
Science, Technology, Engineering, Art & Math

**RED
CHAIR
·PRESS·**

Egremont, Massachusetts

The Jesse Steam Mysteries are produced and published by:
Red Chair Press LLC   PO Box 333   South Egremont, MA 01258-0333
www.redchairpress.com

 FREE Educator Guide at www.redchairpress.com/free-resources

For My Grandson, Liam

Publisher's Cataloging-In-Publication Data
Names: Bowser, Ken, author, illustrator.
Title: The question of the vomit vortex / written & illustrated by Ken Bowser.
Other Titles: Vomit vortex

Description: South Egremont, MA : Red Chair Press, [2021] | Series: A
  Jesse Steam mystery | "Solving Mysteries Through Science, Technology,
  Engineering, Art & Math." | Includes a word list and hands-on
  Makerspace activity. | Interest age level: 008-011. | Summary: "It's a
  breezy new day and along with a tempest in a chocolate milk glass,
  Jesse's presented with a messy new mystery when Dorky Dougy loses his
  lunch while spinning on the merry-go-round. The big question is, why
  did the ballistic barf fling outwardly, as Dougy spun? Read The
  Question of the Vomit Vortex and learn all about these mysterious
  centrifugal and centripetal forces"-- Provided by publisher.

Identifiers: ISBN 9781643710006 (library hardcover) | ISBN 9781643710013
  (paperback) | ISBN 9781643710020 (ebook)

Subjects: LCSH: Vomiting--Juvenile fiction. | Rotational motion--Juvenile
  fiction. | Merry-go-round--Juvenile fiction. | CYAC: Vomiting--Fiction.
  | Rotational motion--Fiction. | Merry-go-round--Fiction. | LCGFT:
  Detective and mystery fiction.

Classification: LCC PZ7.B697 Qu 2021 (print) | LCC PZ7.B697 (ebook) | DDC
  [Fic]--dc23

LC record available at https://lccn.loc.gov/2020934644

Copyright © 2021 Red Chair Press LLC
RED CHAIR PRESS, the RED CHAIR and associated logos are registered
trademarks of Red Chair Press LLC.

All rights reserved. No part of this book may be reproduced, stored in an
information or retrieval system, or transmitted in any form by any means,
electronic, mechanical including photocopying, recording, or otherwise
without the prior written permission from the Publisher. For permissions,
contact info@redchairpress.com

The publisher is not responsible for websites (or their content) that are not
owned by the publisher.

Printed in the United States of America

0920 1P CGS21

Table of Contents

Cast of Characters

Jesse Steam

Amateur sleuth and all-around neat kid. Jesse loves riding her bike, solving mysteries, and most of all, Mr. Stubbs. Jesse is never without her messenger bag and the cool stuff it holds.

Mr. Stubbs

A cat with an attitude, he's the coolest tabby cat in Deanville. Stubbs was a stray cat who strayed right into Jesse's heart. Can you figure out how he got his name?

Professor Peach

A retired university professor. Professor Peach knows tons of cool stuff and is somewhat of a legend in Deanville. He has college degrees in Science, Technology, Engineering, Art and Math.

Emmett

Professor Peach's ever-present pet, white lab rat. He loves cheese balls, and wherever you find The Professor, you're sure to find Emmett— even though he might be difficult to spot!

Clark

Jesse's next-door neighbor and sometimes formidable adversary. Clark Johnson is always with his slippery, slimy, gross-looking pet frog, Lewis. Yuck.

Lewis

Clark Johnson's slippery, slimy, gross-looking, giant pet frog, who lives in Clark's front pocket and goes everywhere that Clark goes. Yuck, yuck, and more yuck.

Dorky Dougy

Clark Johnson's three-year-old, tag-along baby brother. Dougy is never without his stuffed alligator, a rubber knife, and something really goofy to say, like "eleventy-seven."

Liam LePoole

A black belt in karate, and also the captain of the Deanville Community Swimming Pool Cannonball Team. Liam's best friend is Chompy Dog, his stinky, gassy, and frenzied brown Puggle.

Chompy Dog

Liam LePoole's very best friend and constant companion. Chompy is Liam's stinky, gassy and frenzied, little brown Puggle goes everywhere that Liam goes.

Kimmy Kat Black

Holder of the Deanville Elementary School Long Jump Record, know-it-all, and self-proclaimed future member of Mensa. Kimmy Kat Black lives near the Spooky Tree.

The Town of Deanville

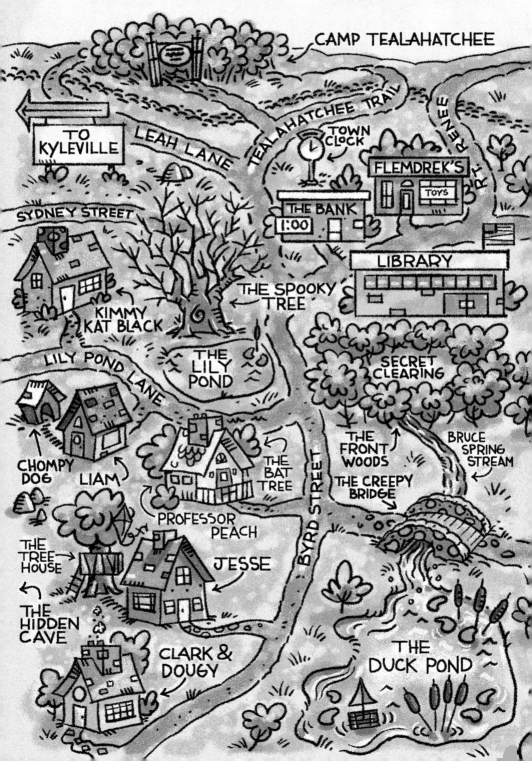

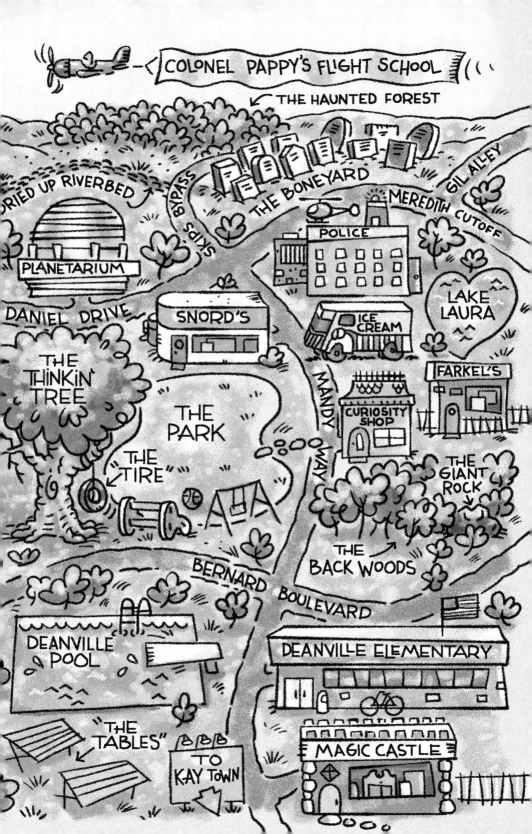

Spin Cycle

Chapter 1

Jesse stood and watched through the window in her bedroom while Mr. Stubbs curled up on his usual spot—the bright sunbeam that spread across the quilt on Jesse's bed like a warm hug.

The birds chirped, the bees buzzed, and the voice on Jesse's clock radio broadcast its blustery prediction. "It's going to be a windy day here in Deanville folks," the voice announced with authority. "So hang on to your hats!"

The breeze outside twirled, and the wind whipped around, creating a whirlwind that spun a gust of leaves in through the open window, without warning—all over Jesse and through all parts of her bedroom.

With that, Stubbs stood, arched his furry back, and stretched.

"Yikes! I wasn't expecting that," Jesse said while laughing to Stubbs. She looked up at her bedroom window as leaves continued to circle into the room and through her billowing bedroom curtains.

The wind finally decided to subside, but by this time, leaves had infiltrated every

corner of her bedroom and clung comically to Stubbs' fur.

"That was like a whirling dervish!" Jesse chuckled to Mr. Stubbs, partly under her breath. "We learned about dervishes during our World Culture Class last month," she went on to explain. "I've never seen anything spin so fast." She laughed.

Tree Trash Trepidation

Chapter 2

Jesse spent the next twenty minutes picking leaves out of her hair, off of Mr. Stubbs, and from what seemed like every corner of her bedroom. Stubbs looked on, showing very little concern, and just continued to lick the back of his paw as if nothing had happened.

"I don't know what that was all about," Jesse talked to Stubbs as she cleaned. "But whatever it was, it sure came out of nowhere." Stubbs looked on.

"Vortex."

Jesse heard a familiar voice coming in from her still-open window.

"What?" Jesse asked as she turned to see Kimmy Kat Black peering through the window from outside.

"It was a vortex," Kimmy proclaimed in her usual, know-it-all manner.

Kimmy Kat Black had a uniquely distinctive way of acting as if she knew everything there ever was to know about everything—always.

"Well, Jesse," Kimmy went on in her own Kimmy Kat way, "as a super genius and a future member of Mensa, I try to keep up with everything atmospheric—like vortexes. Or, vortices if you prefer."

Jesse looked at Kimmy Kat Black as if she had kumquats growing on top of her head.

"Don't look so confused, Jesse. A small cyclone like the one you recently witnessed, or 'vortex' as I referred to it earlier, is simply a mass of whirling air created by certain favorable atmospheric conditions."

Jesse looked at Kimmy Kat Black again as if the kumquats were now full-sized grapefruits. "What are you talking about this time, Kimmy?" Jesse asked confused.

"A vortex, Jesse. V-O-R-T-E-X," Kimmy

spelled it out this time just to be extra snarky. "Try to keep up," she snarked.

"A vortex or cyclone or dust devil, as some may call it, can form when a pocket of hot air near the surface of the earth rises quickly through cooler air above it. That forms an updraft. If conditions are just right, it can begin to spin or rotate. That flow causes more hot air to speed up, moving horizontally and inward toward the bottom,

forming a vortex. They can get pretty big, but they're not like a huge tornado."

Sometimes Kimmy Kat Black didn't know when to shut up.

"That's what just blew past your window a minute ago, causing you all of this tree trash trepidation."

"Tree trash trepidation?" Jesse looked at Kimmy again, even more confused than ever.

"These leaves, Jesse. All of these leaves," Kimmy repeated. "Try to keep up."

The Mighty Messy Milk Malfunction

Chapter 3

At about this time, Jesse had just about all she could stand of Kimmy Kat Black and her snide, "I'm-smarter-than-you" attitude, and she left her room for a snack.

"I'm done with all of this leaf, cyclone, vortex bologna," she snapped back. "I'll be in the kitchen if you guys need me," she advised Kimmy and Stubbs as she walked away mumbling something about chocolate.

As it turns out, chocolate was something Jesse Steam thought about quite a bit.

Chocolate cake was a favorite. Chocolate ice cream—always a hit. And you couldn't go wrong with a good, old-fashioned chocolate bar. But Jesse's true weakness was chocolate milk. A tall, cold, yummy, delicious glass of extra thick, extra chocolatey, chocolate milk.

Jesse opened the cupboard door and

pulled down a large container of cocoa mix. "Ahh! The *pièce de résistance*," she said in a silly French accent as she looked over her shoulder to see Kimmy and Mr. Stubbs trailing her into the kitchen.

"That means, *'the best part'*—or something like that," Jesse informed the two as she turned back around to add the mix to a large pitcher of milk.

"Don't you think I know that?" Kimmy snapped back. "I'm fluent in all of the Latin languages—including Pig." Jesse ignored her.

"Six scoops should do it," Jesse said as she measured out the mix that she was dumping into the large container of milk.

"Extra chocolatey. That's just how I like it," she explained as she continued to dump heaping scoops of mix into the milk pitcher.

Next, Jesse began to stir rapidly with a gigantic wooden spoon. "This is my own personal recipe," she said as she stirred

vigorously with both hands.

Jesse stirred the chocolatey concoction faster and faster. "Ya gotta make sure it's mixed up really, really well," she explained. Glops of chocolate milk began to slosh from the sides of the pitcher as the scrumptious brew began to blend.

"Proper and complete amalgamation and agitation of the ingredients appears to be the key to the ultimate success of this complex formula," Kimmy Kat Black observed in

a fast, monotone voice. She looked over Jesse's shoulder as Jesse stirred.

"Why in the world do you have to make everything sound so darn complicated, Kimmy? Talk about..." Jesse mumbled as she continued to

whip the chocolate milk mixture around in the now-wobbling pitcher.

The faster Jesse stirred, the more rapidly the chocolate milk spun within the walls of the giant milk pitcher. Suddenly, humongous glops of the cocoa concoction began to fling out of the unstable milk pitcher in all directions.

Jesse pulled the spoon from the pitcher, and the chocolate milk continued to spin in the pitcher as if it had a life of its own.

"Inertia!" Kimmy Kat Black yelled out. "Check it out, Jesse! The chocolate milk keeps spinning on its own! That's called inertia," Kimmy blurted.

The two girls looked on as the vortex of spinning chocolate milk continued to twirl in the wobbling pitcher.

The milk continued to spin and spin and spin and the pitcher continued to wobble until...

Here's Mud in Your Eye. And on Your Shirt

Chapter 4

Once Jesse and Kimmy had finished cleaning up the giant mess caused by the "Colossal Chocolate Concoction Catastrophe," as it later became known in Deanville folklore, the two of them prepared to spend the rest of the day at the park. Three of them, counting Stubbs.

The sun was out and shining brightly. Birds sang their happy songs as Jesse and Kimmy Kat Black took to their bicycles for the short ride over The Creepy Bridge to the park by The Thinkin' Tree. A red bird frolicked and bathed in a puddle that was left over from the spring rain that had drenched Deanville the night before.

"I'll race you over the bridge!" Kimmy called out to Jesse as the two pedaled frantically and as fast as they could.

Jesse was the first to come careening down to the bottom of the bridge, and before she could swerve away, she splashed directly through a humongous puddle of muddy, cruddy water.

Pedals whirling. Tires spinning. Birds flying and mud flinging. Jesse raised her feet up from the pedals as she splashed through the puddle—sludge spinning off of her tires in all directions. Mud ran up her back from her back tire and up to her face and front from her front tire. Even Stubbs wasn't spared from the messy onslaught.

Kimmy broke out in laughter as she came pedaling up. Jesse and Stubbs were now thoroughly soaked, head-to-toe, in gross, disgusting, muddy puddle water. "Ah! Centrifugal force at its finest!" Kimmy said as she came coasting to a stop.

"How did I know you were going to have something irritating to say?" Jesse complained as she squeegeed mud off of her cheeks with her fingers.

"Okay. Go ahead, Kimmy. I know you're just itching to give me some irritating explanation of what just happened," Jesse mumbled as she cleaned the last bit of mud off of herself and Mr. Stubbs with her bandanna.

"Well," Kimmy said, "when your tires spun, they created something called centrifugal force. A force that acts outwardly on something moving around a center—like the mud stuck on your spinning tire. If the force is stronger than the mud is sticky, then the mud flies off—outwardly! Simple! It's inertia all over again!"

"And you're annoying all over again," Jesse mumbled under her breath.

Topsy Turvy Tummy Turning

Chapter 5

Looking at the Deanville town map, you'll find that the park is bordered by The Thinkin' Tree to the west and by the back woods to the east. On the north end of the park, you'll notice Snord's Service Station—home to "soda pop so cold, it'll crack yer dang teeth." Then, to the south of the park, you'll see Deanville Elementary School and The Deanville Community Pool. Smack dab in the middle of the park is where you'll find the merry-go-round—and that's precisely where Kimmy, Jesse, and Stubbs were headed.

"I can't remember a time when the merry-go-round was not the cool place to hang out," Kimmy mentioned to Jesse as the trio rounded the corner just beyond The Thinkin' Tree.

It was a beautiful spring afternoon in
Deanville, and the park was especially busy,
just as you would expect.

Clark and Dougy Johnson were there.
Of course, Clark's pet bullfrog, Lewis,
was not far away. Liam LePoole was there,
accompanied by Chompy Dog—his always
gassy pet puggle. "A certified fart machine,"

as the kids often called Chompy.

Clark just happened to be the center of attention and the source of a lot of laughter as Jesse and Kimmy arrived.

"Faster, Dougy! Faster!" Liam coaxed Dougy on as he pushed the merry-go-round as hard as he could with Clark clinging on as tightly as his hands would allow. His

knuckles becoming pale as he gripped the metal bar on the merry-go-round with all of the strength he could muster.

Holding on tightly, Clark spun and spun and spun on the playground merry-go-round. Then Jesse, Kimmy, and Liam all joined in on the pushing. The kids pushed Clark around faster and faster and faster.

Suddenly, Clark wasn't feeling so very great. His eyeballs crossed. He started to sweat. His cheeks puffed out as he held his breath, and his stomach began to churn. Then, his face turned a weird shade of green as the world began to feel topsy-turvy. That's when it happened—"The Great Deanville Playground Vomit Vortex!"

Without warning, everything that Clark had for dinner the night before, the breakfast he had just that morning, and his lunch from only an hour ago decided to make a quick exit from Clark's now queasy belly.

BARF! Last night's cheese pizza came flying out as if it were sprayed from a fire hose.

BARF! This morning's waffles and syrup came spinning out like rancid pancake batter.

BARF! The hot dog that Clark downed for lunch, just an hour earlier, came splurting out with the same runny-gooey consistency as the ketchup and relish that he had squirted on top.

But something mysterious happened that day that remained a conundrum.

While Clark's unfortunate sour shower covered everything BEYOND the merry-go-round, not a single drop had fallen ON to the merry-go-round itself. Or on Clark!

Yes, it was quite the mystery.

Or was it?

I Think That I Shall Never See a Place as Quiet as The Thinkin' Tree

Chapter 6

Jesse always found solace and tranquility within the branches of The Thinkin' Tree.

An ancient Sycamore, or Platanus occidentalis, as Professor Peach referred to it, The Thinkin' Tree was far more than just a tree to Jesse Steam. It was a place of comfort. It's where she went all on her own, to sort out her deepest feelings—both good and bad.

The Thinkin' Tree was where Jesse went to be so thankful on the day that her dearest friend, Mr. Stubbs, strayed his way into her life. It was also where she went to find comfort on the day that she was rejected from a part in the school play. Something that she really wanted—really badly.

Yes. The Thinkin' Tree.

Jesse could be found here frequently,

hanging upside down from its limbs, contemplating all things that required deep introspection.

"When I hang upside down here, gravity pulls all of my best thoughts and ideas down into my brain," she would often say to Mr. Stubbs, who was always close by.

Jesse hung from the tree in her normal position. Stubbs slept below, curled up next to Jesse's messenger bag, near her bike.

Jesse felt badly for Clark. *Nobody likes to be sick,* she thought. Although she couldn't help but laugh about it just a little bit. After all, it was pretty comical, and no one really got hurt.

She thought about all of the crazy events of the day: the leaves spinning into her room like a tiny cyclone, the chocolate milk tempest in the milk pitcher with Kimmy Kat Black, and the mud-spinning-tire phenomenon.

And now this, "The Great Deanville Playground Vomit Vortex." Jesse couldn't help but think that something bigger must be at play here.

Jesse wondered. "There must be something weird going on in the Universe!" she yelled out loud to herself and down to Mr. Stubbs as she dangled.

"Ah! The Universe really is one weird and wonderful place, my dear," a voice echoed back up to Jesse.

Jesse looked down only to see Professor Peach standing below her. Professor Peach was Jesse's next-door neighbor. He was a retired college professor who held advanced degrees in Science, Technology, Engineering, Art, and Math. If you ever had a question about something complex, he was the one to go to.

"What has you so discombobulated this fine day, Jesse?" The Professor asked.

The Professor was always using big words like discombobulated.

"I don't know, Professor," Jesse answered back to him as she slid down from her perch in The Thinkin' Tree.

"Today has been a series of strange happenings. One weird thing right after another," Jesse explained to The Professor.

They talked about the leaves in her room, the twirling chocolate milk, and the mud

flying off of her tire in all directions. And now, Clark's unfortunate stomach-turning experience on the merry-go-round.

"I just can't help but think that there must be something weird going on in the Universe," Jesse explained to him in a frustrated voice.

"Well, Jesse, in a way, you're right! There are some very interesting and

seemingly unexplainable things going on in the Universe. But nothing that can't be understood with a little insight into some of the very basic forces of nature," The Professor explained.

"Come by tomorrow with your friends, and I'll give you all a lesson in centripetal and centrifugal forces."

"By the way," The Professor pointed out, "If you look closely, you'll notice the word 'center' trying to sneak its way into those two interesting words."

"Centripetal? Sounds like a bug to me." Jesse laughed.

Peach's Porch Proves Perfectly Positioned

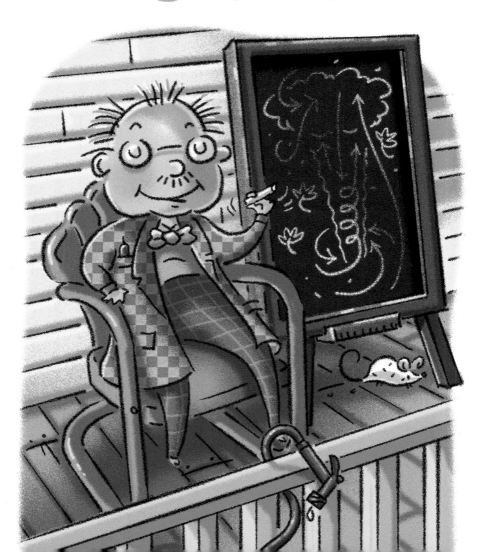

Chapter 7

The next morning arrived, and Jesse and the rest of the gang found themselves positioned on Professor Peach's front porch. He had already begun preparing diagrams on his large chalkboard.

"Who keeps a giant chalkboard around like this?" Clark whispered and chuckled to Liam as the group watched. The Professor continued to prepare the lesson.

"Okay, Kids. Let's start with some basics—like what Jesse and Kimmy Kat Black experienced yesterday," The Professor began.

"Kimmy, you were precisely correct in many of your observations—like the vortex that blew the leaves into Jesse's bedroom window." The Professor drew a diagram of a small cyclone, or dust devil, on the board.

"The sun heated the ground, and that

hot air rose up. As that air rose up and the wind increased, it began to spin—like a top! But unlike tornados, dust devils, like the one Kimmy and Jesse saw, are created from the ground up and are not very big. Generally, they only last for a few minutes. But they sure can blow some leaves around!" The Professor continued to illustrate.

"Okay, let's talk about the tempest in the chocolate milk." He continued to draw.

"Now this, my friends, was a true vortex," he explained. "When Jesse stirred the milk rapidly, it created a tiny cyclone. I encourage you all to try this at home!" He laughed.

"Centripetal force is what kept the milk moving in a circle toward the center of the glass." The Professor demonstrated on the chalkboard and the gang looked on as he drew.

"Now," he said, "the force that flung the mud off of Jesse's tire is entirely different.

"That was not centripetal force at all. It was actually something we call centrifugal force, which is similar but quite different. It's a wondrous and magical thing!

"Centrifugal is the force that seems to pull an object away from the center of something that's turning or rotating." The Professor was getting really excited by this time.

"That's why we feel like we're being pushed to the side when we ride in a car while it turns sharply. Or, why we stay in our seats when we go upside down on a loopty-loop roller coaster. That's centrifugal force!" He laughed.

"So, it's the very same force that caused the mud to fly off of Jesse's tire. It actually 'pulled' the mud away from the rotating center of the tire as it spun!"

As the kids watched, Professor Peach began to do something very curious.

"I have a simple demonstration," he said

to the kids as he worked.

The Professor took a large bucket and tied one end of a rope to the bucket's handle. Then, he filled the bucket to the top with water from his garden hose.

The Professor grabbed the far end of the rope and announced to the group as they watched nervously.

"Ladies and gentlemen and kids of all ages! Observe! As I demonstrate the amazing and mystical powers of centrifugal force!" he proclaimed as if he was a circus announcer.

The Professor took the end of the rope and began to swing the bucket of water back and forth. As the bucket got higher, the kids got more nervous.

"I don't know where he's going with this," Clark whispered to Kimmy Kat Black. "But I don't think this is going to end well."

Suddenly, and with one quick motion, The Professor began to spin the bucket of water

59.

around and around, through the air, and up and over his head! Without spilling a drop!

"Take note! Centrifugal force in all of its glory!" The Professor boasted as he swung the bucket of water over his head, time and time again, without spilling so much as a dribble. The kids looked on in complete amazement.

"Behold! The same forces that kept the water in the bucket are the same forces that sent Clark's projectile puke traveling away from the center of the merry-go-round!"

"I don't know about you, Kimmy," Jesse whispered as The Professor continued frantically with his demonstration. "But I think he's having way too much fun with this..."

The End.

Jesse's Word List

Agitate
to make nervous—*The teacher agitated me with the test.*

Amalgamation
to combine—*The test was an amalgamation of stuff I didn't know.*

Billow
fill with air—*The coach billowed that I had to do more pushups.*

Careen
to move swiftly—*I careen into the lunchroom when I'm hungry.*

Centrifugal
To move from the center—*Read this book to learn more...*

Concoction
a mixture—*My lunch was a concoction of gross stuff.*

Consistency
thickness—*My milk had the consistency of yucky mud.*

Cyclone
rotating wind—*His giant burp came out like a cyclone.*

Demonstrate
to show—*He demonstrated his cyclone-like burp again.*

Discombobulate
confused—*I was discombobulated over his cyclone burp.*

Fluent
able to speak—*He was fluent in cyclone burps.*

Inertia
to continue in a state—*His burps gained inertia with each breath.*

Kumquat
a small citrus fruit—*His nose looked like a kumquat.*

Muster
to assemble—*He mustered ten more cyclone burps.*

Precisely
exactly—*He burped precisely ten more times.*

Projectile
a flying object—*Thankfully, he burped no projectiles.*

Queasy
to feel sick—*His constant burping made me queasy.*

Snide
unpleasant—*I gave him a snide look when he burped again.*

Solace
comfort—*I found solace when he finally stopped burping.*

Tempest
violent wind—*Yes, his burp was like a tempest.*

Vortex
a mass of whirling fluid or air—like his giant burp

About the Author & Illustrator

Ken Bowser is an illustrator and writer whose work has appeared in hundreds of books and countless periodicals. While he's been drawing for as long as he could hold a pencil, all of his work today is created digitally on a computer. He works out of his home studio in Central Florida with his wife Laura and a big, lazy, orange cat.

Try It Out!

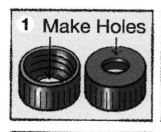

1 Make Holes

2 Top-To-Top

3 3/4 Full

4 Tape

5 Empty

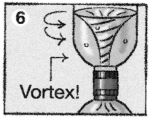

6 Vortex!

Create Vortex in a Bottle!

What You Need: 2 plastic liter-size bottles (including caps), strong tape like duct tape or electrical tape, and water.

Steps:

1. With the help of an adult, put holes in the tops of the caps about as big around as an M&M. It's best to use an electric drill, so be very careful. See diagram 1.

2. Tape the two caps together, top-to-top as shown in diagram.

3. Fill one of the bottles about three-quarters of the way full with water, as shown in diagram 3.

4. Screw one side of the cap onto the bottle with the water in it, as shown in diagram 4. Then screw the empty bottle onto the top of the other cap, as shown in diagram 5.

5. Turn the bottle over using a spinning motion as you set it down, as shown in diagram 6.

Now watch the spinning vortex that you've created!
When the top bottle is empty, you can turn it over and create a vortex over and over again and amaze your friends!